STINGRAY

UNDER FIRE
BY GRAHAM MARKS

B⊞XTREE

The early morning calm was shattered by explosive blasts from a mining platform, out in the Pacific Ocean.

'Hydro-charge force eight - maximum yield, Sir!' reported the gun's operator.

'OK, call up the drag-sweepers and get the mineral on board for processing!' his boss replied.

'Hold it, Sir! I'm getting a strange underwater sounding on my headset!'

'I'm not taking any chances - that cobalt is worth a small fortune - call up the guard patrol sub and get Shore to take a look!'

'HQ to Shore, come in Captain Shore!'

'I'm ahead of you, HQ - I've already picked up the signal.'

But before Captain Shore could speed the guard sub towards the signal, a small alien craft darted out of the depths and fired two rocket torpedoes at the mining stage. With unerring accuracy they shot through the water and exploded on impact with a blinding flash of light, destroying the massive structure.

'World Security Patrol! This is a message from the guard sub with the cobalt mining stage!' Captain Shore yelled into the sub's intercom. 'Am engaging an unidentified hostile craft that has made devastating attack on the platform!'

Speeding through the depths, the squat, finned attacker hugged the narrow, weed-choked crevices in a vain effort to shake off its pursuer. Further and further down they went until the alien sub reached a wide plain, where it darted behind a rocky outcrop and hid.

'Blast! I've lost him!' grunted Captain Shore, as his sleek red craft shot out into the open, his quarry no longer in sight. But before his instruments could register anything, the enemy sub darted out and fired a torpedo

'I'm hit!' exclaimed Captain Shore, as smoke poured into his cockpit and a metal beam fell across his knees, trapping him. 'But I'll ram that sub if it's the last thing I do!'

Struggling with the controls, Captain Shore forced his crippled sub upwards. With a last-ditch effort he careened into the side of the enemy craft. There was another blinding flash...

'Atlanta! Atlanta!!' shouted Commander Shore, as he woke, covered in sweat.

'Father! What's wrong?' asked Atlanta, as she rushed into the bedroom.

'I guess I had a nightmare,' replied her father, turning on his bedside light.

'The submarine wreck…same old recurring dream.'

'Father, wouldn't you like to talk to Troy about it? He'd be only too happy to help.'

'Forget it, Atlanta, I don't want to talk about it - I just need some sleep!'

Atlanta walked out of the room, leaving her father alone with his memories. Unable to sleep, she went into the living room and stood for a while, thinking.Then she reached for the vid-phone.

Five minutes later, Troy was at Commander Shore's bedside,

'Can't a guy have a private nightmare without everyone rushing into his bedroom?' barked the Commander.

'Maybe just talking about this dream will help, Sir.' said Troy. 'Atlanta's filled me in on some of the story,' said Troy, sitting down. 'How you were crippled in that sub disaster, and about the mysterious underwater craft that attacked the cobalt mining stage.'

'That was five years ago…I thought I'd shaken off the dreams, but now they're back!'

'I saw on the news that they've completed a new platform,' said Atlanta.

'Say!' smiled Troy. 'That could be it! The new platform has sparked off the dreams.'

'You should tell Troy the rest of the story, Father…what happened after the explosion.'

'I suppose you're right, Atlanta,' sighed the Commander, lying back. 'It was like this. When I came to, I was lying in a liferaft in the middle of the ocean.

'I tried to figure out how I got there, and then I saw a strange man at the other end of the raft, rowing…he had a kind face and I called him "The Ghost of the Sea".

'Well, I passed out again,' went on Shore, 'and when I came round it was night and I could make out a coastline. The man gave me a sort of half-smile and waved. I looked away for a moment and when I looked back he'd disappeared!

'I drifted to shore,' said the Commander.

'Ended up in hospital in Ecuador…and that's about it.'

'Maybe this guy was the other pilot?' suggested Troy.

'Why should he try and kill me and then save my life?' Shore pondered. 'And you know, it's a funny thing, but that new mining stage starts blasting for cobalt today for the first time in five years.'

'So if the pilot of that other sub did survive, that means he could strike again!' 'But this time Stingray will be waiting,' smiled the Commander. 'We'll get started right away!'

Soon the alert was sounding all over Marineville, its distinctive drumbeat echoing out with the dawn. In the control room, Atlanta checked her instruments, while on board Stingray Captain Troy Tempest gave the order to launch: 'OK Commander, Marina - hold tight! Phones, let's go!'

'Proceed to mining stage,' said Atlanta over the intercom. 'Position south, south west - 1300, reference eight - and good luck with the ghost hunting!'

Some time later, as they were approaching the mining stage, Troy ordered Phones to surface for a look at the new platform.

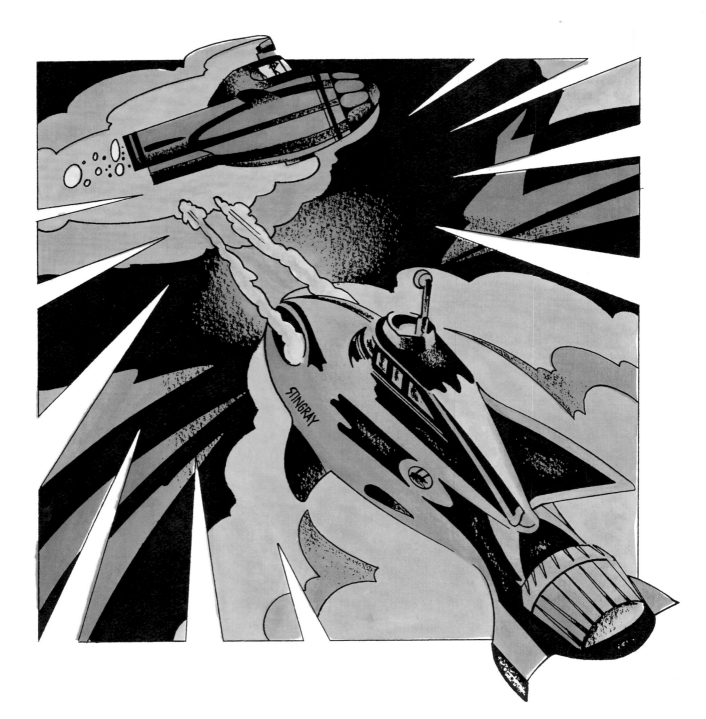

'Hold it!' yelled Phones. 'I'm picking up a signal - it's another craft, quite small...but, yeah - I have it!' he whooped. 'It's just out of range of our Sting missiles at Green 8-zero... and it's moving fast!'

Suddenly, out of the depths, came a small sub. As it sped towards the platform it released two deadly rocket torpedoes. There was nothing the crew on board Stingray could do but watch helplessly as the missiles exploded against the underside of the platform.

'I don't believe it!' cried the Commander, open-mouthed. 'I just don't believe it! It's the nightmare all over again!'

'Not quite, Commander - this time Stingray's here!' said Troy, as he accelerated after the enemy sub.

'It's stopped in the next valley, Troy!' muttered Phones, who was tracking the craft.

'The same ambush position as last time!' growled the Commander.

'Prepare Sting missiles!' said Troy as they entered the valley. 'Fire!' he ordered as soon as he saw the other sub. Sting 1 sped across the ocean floor and exploded right next to the alien sub, which quickly retreated.

As they left the valley, Troy saw that their prey had turned to face them. Without hesitating, he ordered Phones to fire a second Sting missile. This time it hit its mark, blasting the side off the the alien sub. 'We got it!' shouted Troy. He saw the damaged sub disappear into a small, dark entrance at the base of a cliff.

'Take her down, Phones - let's have a look!'

Gliding slowly towards the cave mouth, Troy soon realised that Stingray was too big a craft to get in, 'I'll have to follow it in my diving gear - Phones, drop Stingray onto the ocean floor!'

'You'd better take Marina, Troy,' said Commander Shore. 'This part of the ocean is littered with giant crawling clams - get your leg trapped in one of those and you're as good as dead! Marina will be able to steer you clear of them.'

As they swam, Troy, armed with his harpoon gun, kept his eyes peeled for any danger, but the only thing they saw was the alien sub, illuminated by an eerie blue light, at the end of the tunnel.

Swimming up to the damaged sub, Troy spotted an access port on its underside. Signalling to Marina to follow him, he hauled himself inside.

'A one-man craft and it looks like the bird has flown.' said Troy as they surveyed the interior. Suddenly one of the control panels burst into flames, billowing thick black smoke into the cabin.

'Get out of here fast, Marina!' ordered Troy, pushing her towards the escape hatch. As the flames licked hungrily at the panelling and complex wiring of the enemy sub, Troy and Marina dived for safety out of the hatch - and not a moment too soon! As they swam for their lives, the sub detonated in a ball of flame, sending the two of them hurtling out of the cave mouth.

'The crewman escaped,' explained Troy, once they were back on board Stingray. 'There must be another exit to that cave.'

'OK,' said the Commander, turning to Phones. 'Get ready to search the area!'

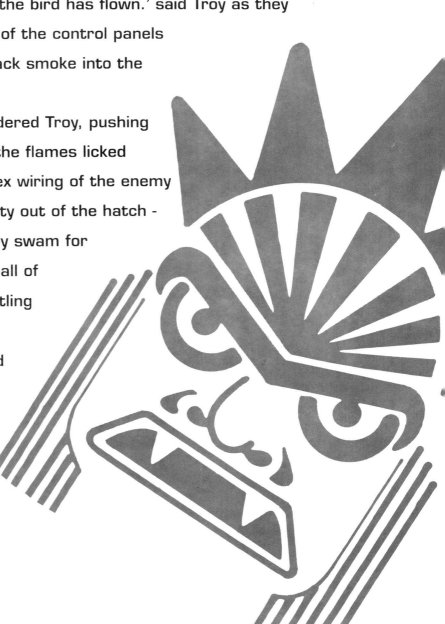

'We won't be able to pick up a man on the sound scanner.' Phones looked out of the cockpit window. 'We're going to have to use our eyes!'

As Troy took Stingray round the outcrop of rock, everyone kept watch.

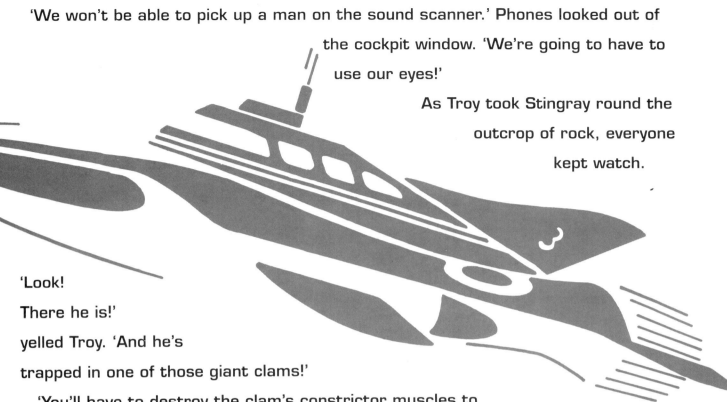

'Look! There he is!' yelled Troy. 'And he's trapped in one of those giant clams!'

'You'll have to destroy the clam's constrictor muscles to release its grip and get him free.' said the Commander. 'Look at his face! It's the guy who rescued me!'

'I told you we'd solve this thing.' grinned Troy. 'Now Phones, take us in as close as you can get.'

Once more in his diving gear, and carrying his harpoon gun, Troy began the dangerous journey through the giant clam beds. As he swam carefully through them they snapped their incredibly powerful shells at him, but his luck held.

Finally Troy reached the old man, who was trapped up to his waist in a particularly huge clam.

'His legs are dangerously close to the constrictor muscle,' Troy thought to himself as he assessed the situation. 'This has to be a good aim or I'll kill him!'

Raising his harpoon gun, and holding his breath to steady his arm, Troy fired at the shell. The needle-sharp harpoon buried itself in the clam and slowly it opened, letting its captive drift free. As Troy watched him swim away, the old man lifted one hand in greeting, and Troy returned the salute.

'He's letting the pilot go!' reported Phones.

'He's what! What's the matter with that guy?' roared the Commander. 'Has he gone crazy?'

'Captain Troy Tempest!' Shore yelled into his microphone as he zoomed across the deck in his auto-chair. 'Return to this ship immediately...I want an explanation, and it had better be good!'

'...And you call that an explanation!' Commander Shore yelled at Troy as he stood to attention in front of him. 'The fact that he saved my life shouldn't have stopped you doing your duty - you should have taken him prisoner!'

'The decision I made was for you,' explained Troy. 'If it was wrong, I take full responsibility.'

The Commander thought it over for a moment. 'Off the record, Troy, what other decision could any man have made?'

'Thank you, Sir,' smiled Troy, relieved. 'I figure this guy won't give us any more trouble - treat people right and it usually pays off.'

'Troy!' shouted Phones excitedly, 'I'm picking up a signal - Green 9-zero! He's heading for us in another sub!'

'What were you saying about treating people right?' scowled the Commander. 'You give a guy a break and see what happens!'

'Fire Sting missile as soon as the craft's in range!' ordered Troy.

'Hold it!' said the Commander as the alien sub came into view. 'They're signalling in international code. They regret attacking the mining vessels and want to establish friendly relations with us. Well, Troy, looks like we made the right decision after all.'

'Yeah!' grinned Troy. 'Guess *we* did!!'

First published in the UK 1992 by BOXTREE LTD, Broadwall House, 21 Broadwall,
London SE1 9PL
1 3 5 7 9 10 8 6 4 2
Copyright © 1992 ITC ENTERTAINMENT GROUP LTD.
Licensed by Copyright Promotions Ltd.
Design and illustrations by Arkadia
1-85283-776-4
Printed and bound in Great Britain by Lawrence Allen, Weston-super-Mare
A catalogue record for this book is available from the British Library